HtENCl4

GALACTIC
GOGGLES

ASTROSNIPS

MICROPLIERS

MEGAMAG MALLET

PLASMA PUMP

ANTIMATTER
HAMMER

ROBOT CLAMP

For Judith  – D. U.

To Mike, who turns stars into constellations  – M. H.

First paperback edition published in 2020 by Chronicle Books LLC.
Originally published in hardcover in 2015 by Chronicle Books LLC.

ISBN 978-1-7972-0833-6
Manufactured in China.

MIX
Paper from responsible sources
FSC™ C104723
FSC
www.fsc.org

Original book design by Kristine Brogno.
Paperback design by Meghan Legg.
Typeset in Geom Graphic.
The illustrations in this book
were rendered with gouache,
brush and ink, graphite, rubylith
and digital process.

10 9 8 7 6 5 4 3 2 1

Chronicle Books LLC
680 Second Street
San Francisco, California 94107

Chronicle Books –
we see things differently.
Become part of our community at
www.chroniclekids.com.

# INTERSTELLAR CINDERELLA

By Deborah Underwood

Illustrated by Meg Hunt

chronicle books·san francisco

**Once upon** a planetoid,
amid her tools and sprockets,
a girl named Cinderella dreamed
of fixing fancy rockets.

She fixed the robot dishwashers
and zoombrooms in her care,

but late each night she snuck away
to study ship repair.

One day her wicked stepsisters
came dashing in, excited.
'The Prince's Royal Space Parade!
Our family's invited!'

'I wish that you could come, my dear.
Alas, no room! Although . . .
why don't you fix that broken ship
and fly it to the show?'

'My toolbox!' Cinderella cried.
'We're stranded here, I guess.'

But Murgatroyd the mouse sent out a cosmic SOS.

'I'm here – your fairy godrobot!
I'll make you brand-new tools.
You'll need a spacesuit, too, of course:
Atomic blue! With jewels!

This power gem will speed your ship
across the starry sky.
It only lasts till midnight –
after that, your ship won't fly.'

'Oh, thank you!' Cinderella said.
She quickly fixed the rocket,
then tucked the sonic socket wrench
inside her spacesuit pocket.

She zoomed past stars and nebulae,
and parked beside a moon.
The space parade was glorious!
Each starship made her swoon.

At last the royal ship approached.
Her heart was filled with yearning.
The ship of Cinderella's dreams!
But what on earth was burning?

The prince's spaceship jerked and hissed
and spewed a cloud of grit.
The prince hopped out. 'Oh blast! What now?
My chief mechanic quit!'

But Interstellar Cinderella
knew just what to do.
She zipzapped with her socket wrench –
the ship was good as new!

The prince invited her aboard.
Last stop? Galactic Hall!
He said, 'I hope you'll join me
for the Gravity-Free Ball.'

They talked for hours of rocket ships,
the time went whizzing by.
Then Cinderella saw the clock
and said, 'I have to fly!'

The prince sent a transmission
to the furthest edge of space.
'I'll search the cosmos for her.
How I wish I'd seen her face!'

'The prince's ship!' Grisilla screeched.
Her sister squealed in fear.
'The prince won't marry one of us
if Cinderella's here!'

Their mother said, 'Don't worry.
He won't find her in this house!
I've trapped her in the attic
with that useless robot mouse.'

The prince's cargo door revealed
a broken craft within.
'The girl I seek can fix a ship.
So – who'd like to begin?'

He gave the sonic socket wrench
to one, then to the other.
Alas, they couldn't fix the ship
(and neither could their mother).

Cinderella struggled,
but the space rope held her tight,
till Murgatroyd's robotic teeth
cut through it with one bite.

'The ship! It's leaving! Wait – what's this?'
She made a fast repair,

then strapped the rusty jetpack on
and blasted through the air.

She landed right beside the prince.
'That wrench is mine!' she cried.

She quickly fixed the ailing ship.
The prince said, 'Be my bride!'

She thought this over carefully.
Her family watched in panic.

'I'm far too young for marriage,
but I'll be your chief mechanic!'

Amid her fleet of sparkling ships,
and friends both old and new,
a joyful Cinderella cried,
'My stars! Dreams do come true!'

ION TETHER

COSMICALIPER

GYRO TORCH

GOOGOL
GAUGE